Watch the Cookie!

Written and Illustrated by
Nancy Cote

Sky Pony Press
New York

To Ruth Beach, my trusted friend
and super talented mentor.

To Harper who loves Mousey, Liam who loves
cookies, and Shea who is a cookie!

To Caroline, my tester-outer.

And finally, to Julie M. who is bigger than a cat,
stronger than a cat, and the purr-fect editor.

With love, N. C.

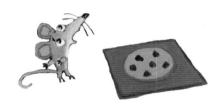

Sky Pony Press books may be purchased in bulk at special discounts for sales promotion, corporate gifts, fund-raising, or educational purposes. Special editions can also be created to specifications. For details, contact the Special Sales Department, Sky Pony Press, 307 West 36th Street, 11th Floor, New York, NY 10018 or info@ skyhorsepublishing.com.

Sky Pony® is a registered trademark of Skyhorse Publishing, Inc.®, a Delaware corporation.

Visit our website at www.skyponypress.com.

10 9 8 7 6 5 4 3 2 1

Manufactured in China, September 2015
This product conforms to CPSIA 2008

Library of Congress Cataloging-in-Publication Data is available on file.

Cover design by Danielle Ceccolini
Illustrations credit Nancy Cote

Print ISBN: 978-1-5107-0309-4
Ebook ISBN: 978-1-63220-232-1

Sam and Mousey were best friends.

When Sam read books, Mousey read, too.

When Sam took a bath, Mousey did, too.

When Sam went to sleep, Mousey slept close.
So close that Sam could barely move.

One morning the wind was blowing hard.

"Let's go to the park and fly my kite," said Sam.

"I'll wait at home," said Mousey, who had never flown a kite.

"Please," begged Sam.

Mousey couldn't say no.

"Hold on tight!"
Sam called as the kite went up and up.
Mousey held on tight.

"I knew you could do it," said Sam when they sat down to rest.

Sam reached into his pocket.

"Surprise!"

he shouted. It was a great big chocolate chip cookie wrapped in a red paper napkin.

Mousey jumped up and down. But then Sam began to wiggle.

He crossed his legs.

He stood.

He rocked
back and *forth.*

Sam couldn't wait.
He had to go.

AND HE HAD TO GO **NOW!**

"Watch the cookie. I'll be right back," he told Mousey.
Mousey gulped. He wasn't the only one watching the cookie.

Two pigeons flew down
and began to peck at the
crisp brown edges.

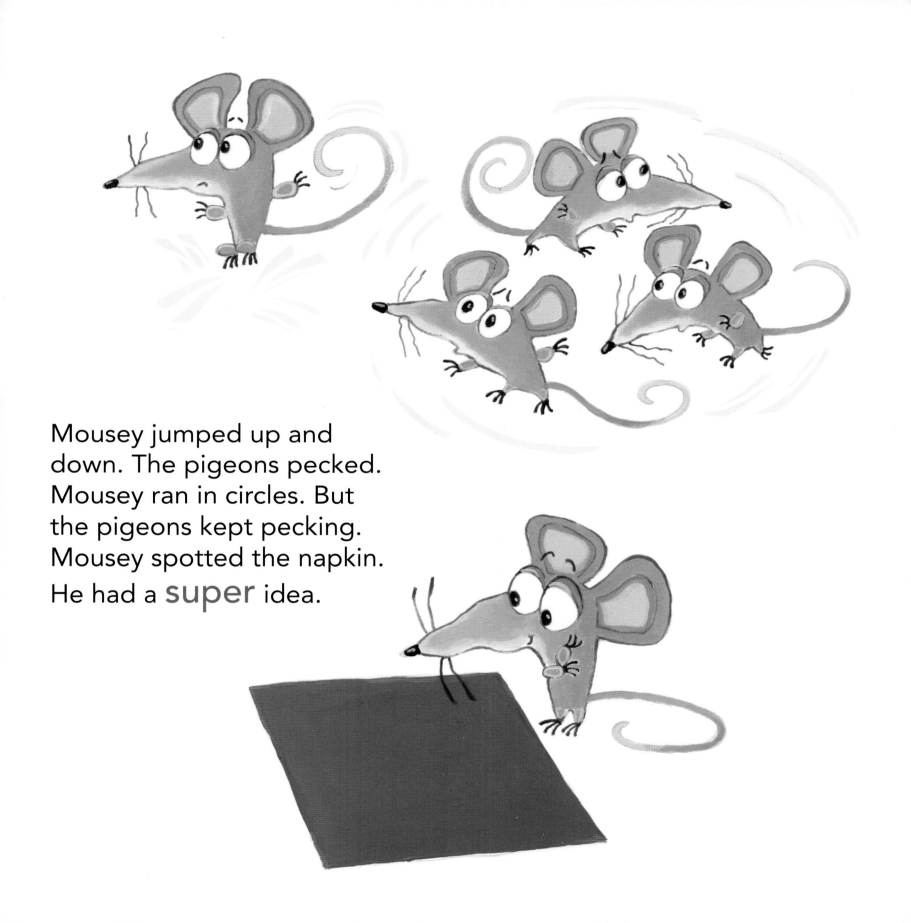

Mousey jumped up and down. The pigeons pecked. Mousey ran in circles. But the pigeons kept pecking. Mousey spotted the napkin. He had a super idea.

"Stop! That's Sam's cookie!" Mousey said with determination.

The pigeons flew away, knocking the cookie to the ground.

An army of ants picked up the cookie and marched.

Mousey stamped his feet. The ants marched.

Mousey waved his arms. But the ants kept marching.

Mousey cleared his throat. He leaped to the ground.

The ants dropped the cookie.

The cookie rolled down the hill,

around the pond,

under a stroller,

"I smell something **good** to eat," said a voice.

Mousey looked up. A hungry cat was peering down at him.

Mousey grabbed the cookie and held it tight.
"That's Sam's cookie!" he squeaked.

"Silly mouse, cats don't eat cookies! Cats eat mice!"

Mousey wasn't strong like a cat.
  He wasn't big like a cat.
  But he had something the cat
didn't have.
  The cat opened his mouth
wide . . .

With super strength, Mousey hurled the cookie into the cat's mouth.

"That's **Sam's** cookie!" he roared.

The cat dropped Mousey and ran away.

Sam saw the whole thing.
"You are very brave," he told Mousey.
"I guess I am," said the little mouse.

"Let's go home and make another cookie," said Sam. "No, let's have a peanut butter sandwich instead," said Mousey.

"Whatever you'd like," answered Sam.

That night,

when Mousey read a book, Sam read, too.

When Mousey took a shower, Sam did, too.

And when **Mousey** went to bed,

Sam slept close. So close that **Mousey** could barely move.

That's just what **best friends** do.